Copyright © 2020 Clavis Publishing Inc., New York

Originally published as *Sam en Bennie en het zwemdiploma*
in Belgium and the Netherlands by Clavis Uitgeverij, 2018
English translation from the Dutch by Clavis Publishing Inc., New York

Visit us on the Web at www.clavis-publishing.com.

Benny Learns to Swim written by Judith Koppens and illustrated by Marja Meijer

ISBN 978-1-60537-497-0 (hardcover edition)
ISBN 978-1-60537-516-8 (softcover edition)

This book was printed in January 2020 at Nikara, M. R. Štefánika 858/25, 963 01 Krupina, Slovakia.

First Edition
10 9 8 7 6 5 4 3 2 1

Judith Koppens & Marja Meijer

Benny
Learns to Swim

Clavis

NEW YORK

Sam and Benny are walking through the woods.

Phew! **It sure is hot today.**

When they get to the lake,

Benny wags his little tail and looks up

at Sam with a question in his eyes.

"No, Benny," Sam says sternly. "You can't swim.
You haven't passed your swim test yet." Benny looks at Sam.
He really just wants to go for a swim. But Sam continues,
"Come on, Benny, I'll show you."
And she turns to head home.

Sam takes Benny upstairs. "Look, Benny," she says.

"This is my swimming certificate.

It means that I can really swim and that

I can go in the pool without water wings."

"Come on, Benny. **We'll go to the pool so you can take swimming lessons,**" says Sam.
"Then you can pass your test and swim in the lake."

"You have to stand in line, Benny,
and listen carefully to the teacher."
Benny wags his tail and stays in line like a good dog.

The swim teacher looks at everyone in line
and stops when he sees Benny.
"What do we have here?" he asks, surprised.
"I'm sorry, but your dog can't join the swim lesson."

"Come on, Benny," Sam softly says.

"I think I know why the teacher sent you away.

You're not wearing a bathing suit.

No one can go in the pool with a bare bottom!

That means you, too. Here, we'll put this on

so you can learn how to swim."

Quietly, Sam and Benny get back in line.
But the teacher sends them away again.

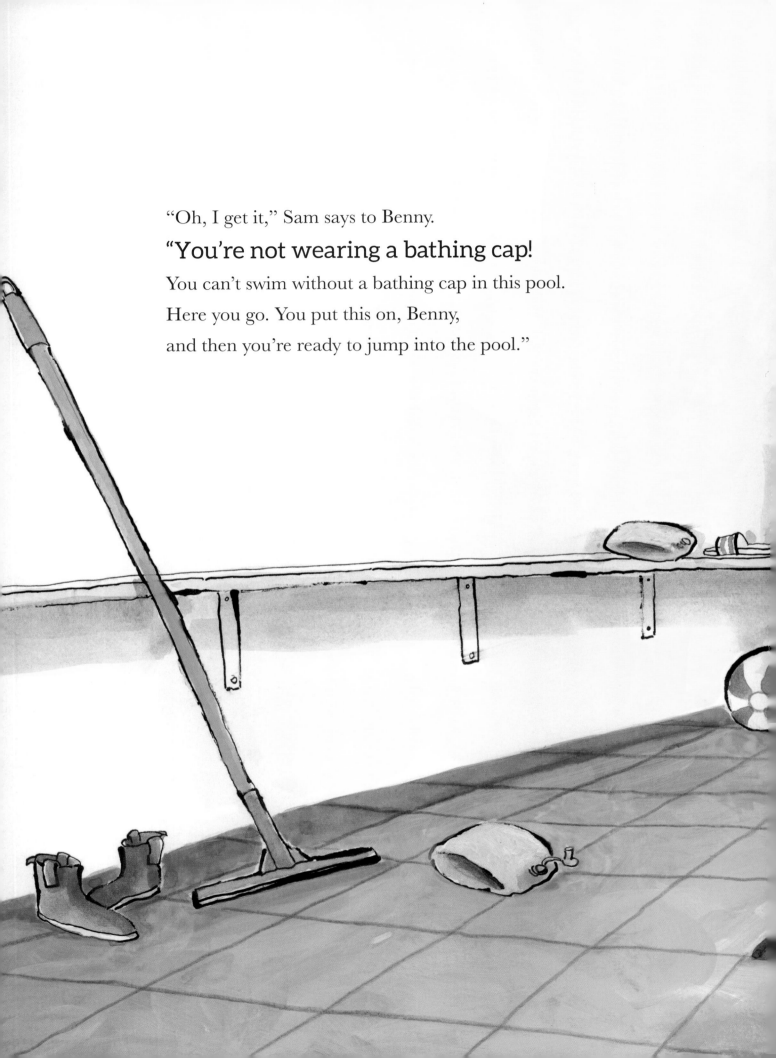

"Oh, I get it," Sam says to Benny.

"You're not wearing a bathing cap!
You can't swim without a bathing cap in this pool.
Here you go. You put this on, Benny,
and then you're ready to jump into the pool."

This time the swim teacher meets them before
they reach the side of the pool. "Why did you
bring your dog to the pool?" he asks Sam.
"Well . . ." Sam starts carefully. "Benny wants
to swim in the little lake in the woods,
but he has never taken swimming lessons.
**And you can't just jump in the water
without lessons.** I want him to pass
his swim test, like me."

The swim teacher laughs. "You know," he says with a kind voice, **"dogs don't need lessons to learn how to swim.** They can swim from the day they are born."

"Really?" Sam asks, surprised.

"Yes," the swim teacher says. "So you can definitely take Benny for a swim.

Just not in the pool. The pool is for people and not for dogs."

Sam and Benny rush to the lake in the woods. Sam throws a branch
in the water and Benny swims right to it and brings it back to her.
She throws the branch again and again. "I have the best dog in the world!"
Sam proudly says. **"Because Benny knows how to swim
without ever taking a lesson!"** Hooray for Benny!